Spiders

Contents

1

The Phobia Clinic

'The Doctor will see you now,'
said the receptionist.

Mick went through to the Doctor's surgery.
It was a large room,
with a deep carpet.
There were potted plants
and pictures on the walls.
It looked pretty smart, thought Mick.
But then, it ought to,
for the money he was paying.

WIRE CHILLERS

Spiders

Brandon Robshaw

Published in association with
The Basic Skills Agency

Hodder

A MEMBER OF

Acknowledgements
Cover: Stuart Williams
Illustrations: Jim Eldridge

Orders; please contact Bookpoint Ltd, 39 Milton Park, Abingdon, Oxon OX14
4TD. Telephone: (44) 01235 400414, Fax: (44) 01235 400454. Lines are open
from 9.00–6.00, Monday to Saturday, with a 24 hour message answering service.
Email address: orders@bookpoint.co.uk

British Library Cataloguing in Publication Data
A catalogue record for this title is available from the British Library

ISBN 0 340 77261 1

First published 2000
Impression number 10 9 8 7 6 5 4 3 2 1
Year   2005 2004 2003 2002 2001 2000

Typeset by GreenGate Publishing Services, Tonbridge, Kent.
Printed in Great Britain for Hodder and Stoughton Educational, a division of
Hodder Headline Plc, 338 Euston Road, London NW1 3BH, by Atheneum
Press, Gateshead, Tyne & Wear

The Doctor was sitting behind a huge desk.
He was a middle-aged man
with glasses, a bald head and a square face.
He got up and held out his hand to Mick.

'Welcome to the Phobia Clinic.
I hope you'll enjoy your stay with us.
Take a seat.
Tell me, what seems to be the trouble?'

'It's – I'm scared of spiders,' said Mick.

'Scared of spiders,' repeated the Doctor.
'Go on.'

'Well, I – I'm not just scared of them.
I'm terrified.
When I see a spider,
I just freeze.'

'I see,' said the Doctor.
'How long have you felt like this?'
'Since I was a little boy,' said Mick.
'Can you help me, Doctor?'

The Doctor smiled.
'Of course.
I've treated dozens of cases like this.
Your treatment will start tomorrow.'

'What *is* the treatment?'

'You'll find out tomorrow,' said the Doctor.
'You just relax for the rest of the day.
Get a good night's sleep.
And don't have nightmares!'

2

Fear of Spiders

At supper that evening,
Mick talked to some of the other patients.
Like him, they had booked into
the Phobia Clinic for a week.
They all had different phobias.
One man was afraid of heights.
A woman was afraid of snakes.
Another woman was afraid of cats.
Nobody else had spiders.

Mick didn't sleep very well.
He went to the Doctor's office
at 9 o'clock the next day.
His heart was beating fast.

'So, spiders,' said the Doctor.
'Tell me your feelings about them.'

'I – I just hate them,' said Mick.
'The way they move so quickly.
Scuttling over the floor on eight legs.

Even the word, 'spider'
– I hate it!
It makes me think of little spying eyes.
Did you know spiders
have got eight eyes, Doctor?'

The Doctor nodded.

'And the way they kill their prey,' said Mick.
'They trap it in their web.
Then they wrap it up so it can't move.
Then they suck its insides out – ugh!'

'I see,' said the Doctor.
'Well, let's see if I can change your mind
about spiders.'
He took out a little box.
'Guess what I've got in here?'

3

Face to Face with Fear

Mick sank back in his seat.
'It's not – it's not –
a *spider*, is it?'

The Doctor leaned forward.
He opened the box.
There, crouched inside,
was a spider.
A big, black spider.

Mick couldn't breathe.
'Please,' he whispered.
'Take it away!'

The Doctor looked at the spider a little
longer.
'They're wonderful creatures, really,' he said.
He closed the box.

'There. You saw a spider.
And nothing bad happened.
You're all right.
That's how the treatment works.
You meet the thing you fear
face to face.

Bit by bit,
you get used to it.'

Mick shuddered.
'I don't think I'll ever get used to it.'

'By the end of the week,
you'll be happy to let the spider
crawl all over you.'

'Don't,' said Mick.
'Don't make me do that.
It'll drive me mad.
It'll kill me!'

The Doctor smiled.
'We'll take it bit by bit.
Tomorrow, I'll take the spider out of the box.'

4

How Did it Start?

It was the next day.
Mick was in the Doctor's office again.

'Tell me,' said the Doctor,
'how did this phobia start?'

Mick swallowed.
'When I was six,
I stamped on a spider.
My mother said the Queen of the Spiders
would come and get me in the night.
She was only joking.
But it terrified me.
It gave me bad dreams.
For years I had bad dreams.'

Mick closed his eyes.

'When I was older,' he went on,
'I read about spiders.
About how they kill their prey.
About how the female spider
eats the male spider.
The dreams got worse.'

'And you still have bad dreams?'
asked the Doctor.

'Yes,' whispered Mick.

'There's nothing to be afraid of really.'
The Doctor took out the little box again.
'Watch.'

He opened the box
and tipped the spider into his hand.
It scuttled over his palm.

The Doctor turned his hand this way and that.
The spider scuttled
from one side to the other.

'You see?' he said.
'Nothing bad happens.
It's quite a nice ticklish feeling.'

Mick didn't answer.
He turned his face away.

'Tomorrow,' said the Doctor,
'you can do this.'

Mick didn't sleep well that night.

5

Eight Dry Legs

Mick stood outside the Doctor's office
the next morning.
His lips were dry.
His palms were sweating.

He swallowed,
knocked on the door
and went in.

'Sit down,' said the Doctor.
'Nervous?'

Mick nodded.

'Don't be.
There is nothing to be nervous about.'

He came towards Mick.
He was holding the little box.

'Put your hand out.'

Slowly, Mick held out his hand.
He was trembling.

'Just tell me if it's too much.
I'll take the spider away at once.
All right?'

Mick nodded.
The Doctor dropped the spider
into his hand.

Mick felt the eight dry little legs
scurrying over his skin.
Panic rose in him.
There was a buzzing in his ears.
He couldn't stand it …

He threw the spider to the carpet.
He stamped on it.

The Doctor looked shocked.
Then he looked annoyed.

'There was no need to do that,' he said.
'That spider had done nothing to you.'

6

The Queen of
the Spiders

Mick was still in a state of terror
when he went to bed that night.
The Doctor was right.
The spider had done nothing to him.
He shouldn't have killed it.
What if the Queen of the Spiders
came to get him?

Of course, he didn't really believe
in the Queen of the Spiders.
But he couldn't stop thinking about her.
He was afraid to sleep.
Afraid to dream.

He lay there in the dark.
The hours passed slowly.
He heard a clock strike twelve.
Then one.
Then two.

Then Mick heard a different sound.
A rustling noise.
There was something in the room.

Mick lay as still as a stone.
But his heart was beating fast.
The noise didn't go away.
He couldn't see anything.
It was too dark.

It's nothing, he told himself.
Just imagination.

Switch on the light
and you'll see it's nothing.

Mick reached over
and switched on the light.
And his heart slammed on the brakes.

There, by the side of the bed,
he saw a spider.
A giant spider.
It was the size of a dog.
It had eight long spindly legs
and a face from a nightmare.

It was the Queen of the Spiders.
Her eight eyes stared at Mick.
Her jaws opened and shut.

7

Trapped

For a long moment,
Mick couldn't move.
Then something snapped.
With a wild cry,
he leaped out of bed.

He ran for the door.
But he didn't get there.

He ran into something soft and sticky.
Something he couldn't break.
He kicked and struggled,
but it was no use.
He was trapped.
Trapped in a giant spider's web.

The Queen of the Spiders
scuttled towards him.
She began to wind a soft thread around him.
Around and around and around.

Mick couldn't move.
He was all wrapped up.
Only his head stuck out.

He felt the spider's mouth parts
moving over his neck.
Then a terrible pain,
as her fangs bit into his flesh.

Now … she'll … eat me,
thought Mick.
She'll … suck out … my insides …

That was the last thought he ever had.

8

A Very Bad Dream

The Doctor waited in his office.
Nine o'clock went by.
Then ten o'clock.

Where was Mick?
Was he too afraid
to carry on with the treatment?

At half past ten,
the Doctor went to Mick's room.
He tapped on the door.

No answer.

He pushed open the door.

Mick was lying in bed, quite still.
The Doctor felt his pulse.
He was dead.

Heart attack,
thought the Doctor.
He must have died in his sleep.

He looked at Mick's face.
The eyes were wide and staring.
The lips were drawn back from the teeth
in terror.

It must have been
a very bad dream,
thought the Doctor.

He sighed.
He pulled the sheet over Mick's face.
Then he left the room to report the death.

28